I0766338

Forgiving Secrets: Leah's Story

Danni Peters

Published by B & F Publishing.

Identifiers:

Canada copyright 1210562
ISBN: 978-1-7782441-2-4 (hardback)
ISBN: 978-1-7782441-3-1
Available in hardback and ebook.

Formatting and Editing by Felicity Fox

Cover Design by: B & F Publishing

Contents

ONE

The sun shone brightly on the clear, calm lake. The reflection on the smooth, still water blinded Leah as she knelt beside it and stared into the water at the serene picture before her. She saw the sun in the blue sky along with some puffy white clouds. The leaves on the trees were a beautiful multi-coloured spectrum of orange, red, and yellow. Autumn was in full swing, and a few leaves fell silently. She looked behind her and saw her beloved dog, Clara, a St. Bernard pup, grinning back at her. The image before her seemed so peaceful until her own distraught and shocked reflection came into her line of vision. Her strawberry blonde hair hung in front of her hazel eyes, red from the tears, and her face was pale. She closed her eyes as she recalled the events of the last hour.

Leah was a woman in her mid-thirties. She would be thirty-six in a few days. She worked in the city as a photographer for a well-known media company, and many of her pictures were in advertisements and other forms of media.

Leah had left home shortly after college and was fortunate to find a job that she enjoyed and in her field of study. Though her parents had passed on, she had a close relationship with her Uncle Jim. Because she had favourable employment, she could periodically return to her hometown to visit him. Jim was a tall man with long blonde hair that he always wore in a ponytail. He always wore jeans and a black T-shirt accompanied by cowboy boots. Though divorced for three years, he moved on despite estrangement from the rest of the family, except Leah, who always visited every few months. The last visit she had with him was when she acquired Clara. Jim had picked up Clara from a local breeder and gave her to Leah as an early birthday gift. She immediately fell in love with the quickly growing St. Bernard pup. Leah took Clara to obedience classes, and the dog accompanied her wherever she went.

Leah sat silently by the water and thought of the last hour's events. When she pulled up to the front of her Uncle Jim's house, everything looked as it always had. The big white house seemed as inviting as usual, the flowers in their last bloom of the season, and the leaves from the big maple trees covered the ground in the yard. The leaves crunched underfoot as she and Clara approached the front porch. They climbed the steps together, but Clara reached the door first and sat down to await Leah's lead.

Leah knocked once and opened the unlocked door because Jim never expected her to wait on the doorstep. She was welcome to enter, and this time, they entered even though Jim's truck was not in the driveway. The house was empty, so Leah took Clara for a short walk to unwind. As they made their way around the house, Leah noticed Jim's truck parked in the far corner of the backyard. It was at the beginning of the path leading through the forest down to the lake on his property.

"Come on, Clara," Leah said. "Let's go and meet Jim at the lake, He must be out fishing." She laughed as Clara headed off down the path. Leah jogged behind her on the well-maintained path. Again, the leaves crunched under their feet. They ran together for about five minutes, then Clara took off quickly ahead of Leah. Leah called, "Clara! Clara, come back." Clara did not listen and disappeared up the hill. Leah heard her barking, ran faster to catch up with her, and saw the reason for the barking. She gasped and stumbled a few steps.

Hanging in the big oak tree that grew at the end of the path at the lake was the limp body of a man. She fell to her knees as the reality of what she saw hit her. The man hanging in the tree was her Uncle Jim.

Two

Leah gasped for breath. Her heart pounded in her chest. She tried to scream, but all she could do was make a muffled moaning sound. She collapsed to the ground in front of the tree. Clara kept on barking and then began to howl. It was evident to both Leah and Clara that Jim was dead. His face was red, his neck was clearly broken, his eyes were bulging out, and his body was limp. "No, Jim! No!" Leah shrieked. She pounded on the ground in front of her. Her body went limp as she passed out from the agony she felt in her heart.

Leah awoke to the feel of Clara gently licking her face. At first, Leah thought that she was dreaming, but the sight of Jim's body hanging in the tree bought her back to the harsh reality.

She got up and forced her eyes away from the gruesome sight in front of her. She dialed 911 on her cell phone. Time seemed to stand still as she waited for the emergency crew to arrive. When an ambulance and four police officers arrived, they found Leah sitting quietly at the shore of the lake. She and Clara stared into the water.

After collecting Jim's body and talking to Leah, the emergency team left. Leah and Clara walked back to Jim's house. There, Leah called her family members and broke the news about Jim's death.

Leah went to her Aunt Kate's house to spend the night. Kate was in her late 40's with red hair and bright green eyes. She was Jim's ex-wife; they had no children of their own. The funeral arrangements would be the following week. For years, Jim's wishes for cremation were clear, and Kate made sure to grant his wish. Leah accepted Kate's request to stay with her until she was ready to go home. Leah spent most of her time there curled up in her bed with Clara, occasionally talking to her other family members on the phone. Since Leah was not in the mood for any company, Kate let her be and checked in occasionally. Leah did, however, manage to take good care of Clara. They went for walks together and spent some time at the dog walking park listening to the sounds of the birds singing their cheerful melodies.

Leah and Kate drove together to the funeral home for Jim's funeral. When they arrived, Leah noticed some brand-new black SUVs. She quietly wondered who they belonged to but didn't give it any more thought then. As Leah entered the funeral home, she was relieved to see that the casket was closed. Jim was a well-liked man, which showed by the number of people who attended the funeral. Leah gave an outstanding and loving eulogy of her Uncle Jim. She went on autopilot and did not get flustered or over-emotional throughout the proceedings.

After the funeral, Jim's lawyer requested that the family remain for the reading of Jim's will. One simple line summed it up: "I leave all my possessions to my niece, Leah." Jim requested that his ashes be spread out in the lake on his property. The funeral director asked Leah to return the next day to retrieve the ashes. When Leah left the funeral home with Kate, she again noticed that the black SUVs were still there. Two men occupied each one. When they spotted Leah, they left, but their appearance slipped her mind as they returned to Kate's house. Clara was there eagerly awaiting Leah's return. Leah hugged Clara, sat down, and cried into Clara's furry shoulder. Later in the evening, Kate and Leah went for a walk with Clara. They shared many good memories about Jim. Even though they had divorced, Kate and Jim had remained friendly towards each other.

Three

The following day, Leah awoke early and got ready to go to the funeral home and retrieve Jim's ashes. Clara was happily waiting to go, as Leah could take her for this. The day was bright and sunny with a gentle breeze. As Leah drove to the funeral home, she noticed how beautiful the colours of the leaves of the maple trees were alongside the road. It was a gorgeous autumn day.

Leah arrived at the funeral home, and the funeral director greeted her. He gave her a small box containing Jim's ashes and offered her a few words of sympathy, and she left. As she walked out of the building to her car, she couldn't help but think, *How could such a vital life be condensed into a small box.* She drove with Clara at her side to Jim's property, *my property*, she thought to herself.

She entered through the unlocked door. The house was very quiet and clean. Jim had always been a good housekeeper, and everything was neat, tidy, and in its place.

Leah almost called out Jim's name but caught herself. Clara followed Leah around the house and out to the front porch. The coloured leaves drifted lazily to the ground in the gentle breeze. The sun shone on Leah's face and she felt the sun's warmth on her skin. Leah and Clara started down the path towards the lake to spread Jim's ashes. The leaves underfoot crunched as they walked along. Clara kept a steady pace alongside Leah.

Leah felt the breeze on her face and smiled for the first time since she had found Jim's body. Clara did not run off ahead this time or bark. It seemed like a normal walk down to Jim's lake. Jim had, in fact, put up a wooden sign that said, "Jim's Lake."

As Leah approached the big oak tree, she felt sadness descend onto her heart. The tree looked as it usually had, dominating the area with its big branches, fewer leaves, and casting a shadow down to the shore of the lake. Leah and Clara followed the shadow and knelt beside the lake. She tenderly took the small box out and held it before her, saying a small prayer for Jim, asking that he receive forgiveness for taking his own life. She then opened the box and poured them about the lake. Leah sat and watched the ashes spread out and finally disappeared into the water.

The sun started to go down, illuminating an orange-pink sunset. Leah realized that she and Clara had spent much of the day by the lake in the beautiful nature setting. They started to head back to the house. The blue solar lights that Jim had lined the path with came on, and the gentle breeze picked up a bit, and it blew Leah's long hair out behind her. Clara kept pace with Leah. They made their way to the house and had dinner. Leah found a well-stocked kitchen and made a healthy meal for herself and Clara. Jim had also stocked up on dog food and treats when he had acquired Clara for Leah.

After dinner, Leah made herself some herbal tea with honey, and she and Clara went outside to sit on the front porch. They got comfortable, sat on the wooden bench swing on the porch, and watched the stars in the moonlight for a while. When they went inside to sleep, they did not notice the SUVs parked a bit down the road, watching the house.

Four

The next morning Leah awoke to a rainy, blustery day. The rain had rolled in as they slept. She got up, showered, and went to make breakfast. Once again, she wanted to call out for her Uncle Jim. But she caught herself and put Clara out for her morning business instead. As Leah looked outside and waited for Clara, she decided to spend the day trying to go through some of Jim's belongings. She still did not know what she was going to do about her inheritance. Leah had not taken a vacation from work for the last few years, so staying at Jim's for the next month was feasible. Leah thought she might leave her city apartment and live in the country. Now, with Jim leaving everything to her, it seemed ideal. She could do most of her assignments from home or would travel for some. A home base in a country setting could work out well. Leah decided to give Jim's clothing and some other items to Goodwill. There were many charities to choose from nearby, so she started packing them up. She worked for a few hours packing boxes before she took a break for lunch. For lunch, Leah went about making herself a sandwich and noticed an envelope on the mantel above the fireplace. She walked into the living room, and when she got close enough to it, she saw the envelope was to her. She carefully opened it and took out the letter. It read:

Dearest, Sweet Leah,

I have left instructions for what to do with my remains. I can't continue living and being part of the cause of so much destruction. I am sorry that I can't face you one more time. I hope you and God will forgive me for choosing to go by myself. Look in the forest and under the big oak tree. I will always love you.

Love, Uncle Jim

Leah read and then re-read the note. Her heart swelled. She still was having a hard time with Jim committing suicide and somewhere deep inside wanted to believe that he didn't. After reading his note, she knew that he chose to end his own life. Leah put the note down, somehow holding the note reinforced Jim's decision. Clara entered the living , and Leah sat down on the floor and cried into her fur. Clara sat down and leaned into Leah's arms. She gently licked Leah's face.

✱ ✱ ✱

Nighttime descended over the area, and Leah again sat on the swing on the porch with Clara. She finished her tea and went inside the guest room but was not ready to sleep in Jim's room. Peering out the window while preparing for bed, she noticed the SUVs down the road. *That is odd. No one lives close around here,* she thought. Most of the surrounding properties were big acreages. It was a good five kilometres in either direction before any houses. She shut the window, pulled down the shade, and felt uneasy about the vehicles. Leah went downstairs and double-checked the locks on the doors, patio doors, and all the windows. Tonight, she even set the alarm. It all seemed strange to her because the doors didn't need locking and usually were unlocked. Leah went back upstairs and went to bed. Clara slept snuggled in at the foot of the bed.

FIVE

Leah had restless sleep and drifted in and out of sleep from nightmare to nightmare. She had horrible dreams of Jim; each dream ended the same way, with the gruesome image of Jim's face hanging from the big oak tree. It was all red and puffy, with bulging eyes, and she heard his voice calling her name. It made her scream, terrified. Every time she woke up, Clara snuggled closer to the head of the bed.

By morning, Clara was on the pillow beside Leah's. The bright sun shone through the window, lighting the wall beside the bed. Leah, awake for the last half hour, decided to get up. She put Clara outside for a while and noticed that the SUVs were gone. She felt more relaxed, showered, and got ready for the day. Leah and

Clara ate their breakfast, and Leah decided to walk to the lake. Before she went, she called a local charity and planned to drop off some things she packed up yesterday.

Before heading down the path, Leah grabbed the note from Jim and a spade shovel. She wasn't sure if she would dig up around the big tree yet but decided to bring it anyway. As she headed down the path with Clara, she did not notice a black SUV pull up across the road and watch her and Clara disappear down the trail.

The birds chirped their happy songs alongside Leah and Clara, visiting the bird feeders Jim had placed along the trail. There was still some seed in them, which Leah would refill on the next walk. They descended the path until they reached the big oak tree. Leah stopped and asked out loud, "Oh, Jim, what do you mean for me to do?" Clara sat by the tree, watching Leah, who patted her on the head. Leah took the spade shovel and started digging around the tree. It wasn't long before she heard the shovel clang against a metal box. She stopped and stepped back, surprised to find something so soon. The box was quite a good size and took several minutes to uncover. She couldn't lift it out of the ground when she tried to pick it up and headed back to the garage to get a cart to bring it back.

Leah and Clara headed back to the house and heard birds chirp, blue jays, chickadees, grosbeaks, finches, and partridge, but every now and then, Leah thought she heard voices but could not decipher if that was true due to the birdsong. Nevertheless, Leah and Clara enjoyed the beauty of nature on their walk back towards the house. At the house, Leah first went into the garage and retrieved a cart and a pry bar to get the metal box out of the ground. Thirsty, she approached the house for water but saw an SUV parked across the road. Two well-dressed men exited the vehicle and walked towards the house. Leah stopped at the front and waited for the men to approach her. Clara was normally a friendly, welcoming dog but stood before Leah this time; her fur stood on her back. Leah noticed Clara's reaction to the two men and instinctively took out her phone, ready to call for help.

The two men made their way to Leah and Clara. Although they smiled and were well-dressed, there was something sinister about them. One of them was taller and well-muscled while the other was short and thin. The shorter one asked her where Jim was. Leah briefly explained that Jim had passed away and asked them why they were looking for him. The tall man looked sternly at Leah and asked, " Where are they now?" Leah had no idea who he was asking about, and she told him so. He looked at her like he did not quite believe her but abruptly turned to leave. He glanced over his shoulder, gave Leah a wicked grin, and said, "I will find them."

Leah felt a shudder run up her spine as she watched the two men leave. Clara growled a low, rumbling growl in her throat as the two men left. Leah wondered what that was all about as she and Clara hurried into the house. The SUV went down the road, out of sight from the house.

Six

As much as Leah wanted to go back and retrieve the metal box, she was concerned about the two men who had visited her. The card the policeman had left was on the kitchen table. Unsure of exactly what to say, the two men did appear menacing, though she wasn't sure why. When she called the number on the card, Leah knew the smooth voice on the other end was Mark Jhar, but she asked for him anyway.

Mark Jhar was a tall, blonde, handsome man, muscular in stature, who reminded Leah of a bodybuilder. He had been on the police force for several years and was well-received by the public. Mark often volunteered to help local agencies and was a part-time volunteer fireman. Among all of this, he also owned a gym and helped train anyone who wanted to get in shape. Jim had been one of his clients for the last few years. Although he had never met Leah, he knew of her from Jim's beautiful stories about his favourite niece. Mark listened closely as Leah told him of her visit from the two men. Because Mark could hear the worry in her voice, he calmly said he would come over and talk to her at the house.

Leah and Clara sat on the porch swing to wait for Mark. When he arrived, Leah offered him coffee before settling on the porch. Leah told Mark again about the visit from the two men and then showed him the note from Jim. Mark was intrigued and asked Leah if she wanted him to accompany her to dig up under the oak tree and look in the forest on the property. Leah accepted the offer; it was evident that Clara liked Mark as she did not growl or bark at him.

After Leah and Mark finished a second cup of coffee, they headed back down the path. Leah explained that she had already dug up under the big oak tree and found a metal box. It was too heavy for her to lift out alone, and she appreciated the help. They talked about Jim and their deep care for him as they walked along. Mark told Leah that he had met Jim at his gym when Jim joined the new weightlifting class. Jim was a lean man who had developed some good muscle tone. Mark and Jim became good friends and often drank coffee after class. Jim had talked much about Leah, so Mark felt he knew her.

Clara walked ahead of Leah and Mark, comfortable with Mark so as not to feel she had to stay right at Leah's side. The birds did not seem to mind the company as they fluttered beside them and sang their birdsongs.

When Leah, Mark, and Clara arrived at the big oak tree, the metal box was still in the ground, just as Leah had left it. Mark and Leah both took ahold of the metal box and dragged it up out of the ground. Mark took ahold of the pry bar and opened the metal box. They both gasped in shock at the contents.

SEVEN

Leah and Mark looked at each other in awe. The metal box was full of primarily gold bars and some silver bars. Inside was also an envelope with a note inside and receipts from the gold and silver bars. The note explained how Jim had used his winning lottery ticket to purchase the bars and buried them under the oak tree for safekeeping. It also went on to say that he intended to give the gold and silver bars to Leah upon his death. Leah could not believe her eyes. *No wonder the metal box was so heavy*, she thought. Leah and Clara stayed at the oak tree as Mark returned to the garage to retrieve a cart to haul the metal box back to the house. Together, they loaded up the cart and made their way back.

Back at the house, they counted the bars. There were twenty-five silver bars and fifty gold bars. They laughed out loud at how much the currency was worth. Mark carefully checked all the receipts to make sure everything was legit. It all looked like Jim had, in fact, paid for every ounce of gold and silver. Leah asked Mark if he would go to the bank with her. She did not want to have all of the bars sitting in the house. Her head spun with that much currency. Another thought entered her mind as she remembered her visitors from the morning. *Could this have been what they were after?* She spoke her concerns aloud to Mark. Mark agreed that it was a good possibility that they were.

Mark and Leah loaded Mark's truck and then headed for the bank. The bank was pleased to have Leah's business and put the bars into the vault for safekeeping. On the way back to the house, Leah remembered that the two men had asked where *who* was, not *what*. It seemed to Mark that perhaps they were not there for the treasure but for something else. They made plans to start searching through the forest on the property the next day after Mark finished work.

✳ ✳ ✳

The following day, Leah and Clara walked down the path to Jim's Lake. They spent the morning planting flowers under the oak tree and installing solar lights around it. She still didn't quite know how she would spend the small fortune that her Uncle Jim had left her. But right now, she knew that she would move onto the property and keep the memory of Jim alive.

Clara ran about and played in the lake while Leah finished gardening. Leah was getting excited to start searching through the forest with Mark. She couldn't imagine what other secrets Jim had been hiding. She ran the suicide note through her mind. "What does he think that I couldn't forgive him for?" She thought out loud. Clara turned her head sideways and looked at Leah as if to agree with her. Then Clara barked happily.

The two then set off back to the house. Along the way, Leah kept her eyes open for anything strange, darting her eyes left and right. The wind had picked up, the remaining leaves in the trees rustled, and the ones on the ground crunched underfoot. The birds chirped, and Leah again didn't hear the sounds of someone calling out. She thought it was only the birds.

When they returned to the house, Leah made lunch and fed Clara. She stayed inside, packing up more of Jim's belongings. Leah did not notice the two men in the SUV driving by her house periodically during the afternoon. When Mark called to say that he would be over shortly, Leah and Clara went and sat on the bench swing on the porch and waited for him.

Eight

When Mark had finished his shift, he went home and changed into civilian clothing: jeans, a hooded sweatshirt, and a pair of hiking boots. He looked forward to another hunt. After what they'd discovered the day before, Mark prepared for anything. Also, he was happy to spend more time with Leah and Clara. As he was about to leave, he recalled recent reports of wolves hanging around the outskirts of Youngston and secured his revolver on his person for peace of mind.

He left his apartment and drove towards Leah's place. When he got closer to her house, he met a black SUV and remembered what Leah had said, so Mark wrote down the out-of-state license plate. *It may come in handy later*, he thought to himself. As he pulled up to Leah's house, he saw Leah and Clara waiting for him on the front porch. She waved and came down the front steps to greet him. Clara happily jumped up and down around Mark. It was evident that she liked and trusted him. Leah was also glad to see him. She felt a pang of attraction for this handsome man.

Both were anxious to start the search through the forest on the property. They decided to bring the shovel and the cart, just in case. As they headed down the path, they looked for anything unusual.

Mark noticed that beside every solar light was a small pile of white rocks. Then he saw one solar light had no stones beside it. As they stopped and peered through the bushes behind it, it looked like someone had deliberately hidden a path behind that solar light.

Their mutual excitement grew as they carefully stepped through the bushes and onto a smaller path. Jim had many lilac trees planted along the main path, and there were more here planted closely at the beginning of the smaller path. The lilac bushes still had their leaves and made the perfect cover.

Clara followed Leah and Mark down the path. They walked for about ten minutes until Clara passed them and ran ahead. Leah remembered the last time that Clara had run off ahead and could feel herself getting very anxious. Leah, suddenly very nervous, her heart thudding, told Mark about the last time Clara had ran off ahead was when she found her Uncle Jim hanging in the big oak tree.

Mark reassured her that he was with her to handle whatever happened. Mark also sensed that it might not be okay but hurried down the path after Clara, who was out of sight around a curve in the path.

Clara's bark led them to her. As they rounded the curve, they saw Clara barking at the door of a cabin. The cabin was a shock because of all the years of visiting Jim. Leah never knew the cabin existed!

NINE

Mark reached the cabin first and waited for Leah, who called Clara back from the door. Mark knocked on the door and called out. They heard someone shuffling around inside. The door slowly opened, and Mark and Leah were shocked to see seven young women inside. They all looked scared to see Mark and Leah. Clara pushed her way inside and gently approached the women. One woman asked them what was happening and wanted to know what they would do to them. The other women remained silent.

Leah and Mark sensed that they were afraid. Because of his training, Mark remained calm and asked them to explain why they were there. One by one, they told similar stories of how they had been kidnapped and held there against their will. They were afraid to try and escape as they were all immigrants into the country and learned that bad behavior would mean their deaths. One woman told of how she had been the second girl at the cabin. The first girl, who was no longer there, had tried to escape and had been killed. As they told their stories, Leah felt sick. Mark called for backup at the cabin, and other police officers arrived to help sort out the mess.

Eventually, all the women went to the police station later to return to their homes. Leah, Mark, and Clara slowly walked back to the house. When they arrived, Mark made Leah a cup of herbal tea. They sat on the porch as Leah talked about her feelings about what she had just discovered about her Uncle Jim. She now understood why he could not face her. Her heart was troubled about why Jim would be involved in such a crime. They sat on the porch swing, the same black SUV as before pulled up. Mark told Leah to go inside with Clara. The two men got out of the SUV and came up on the porch. Again, they demanded to know where the women were but did not know Mark was a police officer and were shocked when he arrested them.

***

Two weeks later, Mark was out on patrol and saw the other two Black SUVs that were at Jim's funeral. He and his fellow officers were able to catch them after a lengthy chase and arrest them.

Leah felt better after hearing that all the men involved were in jail. She still was trying to manage her feelings about her Uncle Jim. The good memories between the two helped to settle her grief over his extra-curricular activities. She understood now why he chose to end his own life, but it still bothered her. Clara stayed by her side, loving and comforting her in her special way. She licked away her tears when she cried and slept snuggled up beside her at night. Mark also frequently visited to check in on her. It was apparent to both that they had real, genuine feelings for each other. Mark was confident that he had met his future wife.

***

One year later, Mark and Leah married and made Uncle Jim's property their home. Clara had also become close to Mark and accepted that it was now to be the three of them forever. Leah and Mark decided to do something good for the community and used some of their small fortune to start up an apartment complex to help wayward souls in need of assistance. Leah also donated money to help people grieving the death of a loved one to suicide.

Two years later, Leah and Mark welcomed their first child and got another dog to keep Clara company. During this time, Leah had been able to forgive her Uncle Jim of his deeds; even though she disagreed with what he had been a part of, she did for herself and her new family. Mark and Leah had found their happily ever after.

Peter 4: 8

Most important of all, continue to show
deep love for each other, for love covers a
multitude of sins.

**If you or someone you know is thinking about
suicide, call or text 9-8-8.**

Suicide helpline in Canada.

**Support is available 24 hours a day, 7
days a week.**

Other Books By Danni Peters